This book is for
LYRA SOFIA,
with love.

U. K. Le G.

A RIDE ON THE RED MARE'S BACK

TWO OCEAN BOOKS

This book belongs to
Emily Kathryn Booth

a gift from her friends,
Josie and Anna

May 11, 2000

A RICHARD JACKSON BOOK

A RIDE ON THE RED MARE'S BACK

by Ursula K. Le Guin

paintings by Julie Downing

ORCHARD BOOKS NEW YORK

Orchard Books, 95 Madison Avenue, New York, NY 10016

Manufactured in the United States of America. Printed by Barton Press, Inc.
Bound by Horowitz/Rae. Book design by Mina Greenstein.
The text of this book is set in 14 point Weiss Roman.
The illustrations are watercolor paintings, reproduced in full color.
Hardcover   10   9   8   7   6   5   4   3   2
Paperback   10   9   8   7   6   5   4   3   2   1

Library of Congress Cataloging-in-Publication Data
Le Guin, Ursula K., date. A ride on the red mare's back / by Ursula K. Le Guin ;
paintings by Julie Downing.   p.   cm. "A Richard Jackson book"—
Summary: With the aid of her magic wooden horse, a brave girl travels to the High House
in the mountains to rescue her kidnapped brother from the trolls.
ISBN 0-531-05991-X (tr.) ISBN 0-531-08591-0 (lib. bdg.) ISBN 0-531-07079-4 (pbk.)
[1. Fairy tales.   2. Trolls—Fiction.   3. Brothers and sisters—Fiction.]
I. Downing, Julie, ill.   II. Title.   PZ8.L47544Ri   1992   [E]—dc20   91-21677

ILLUSTRATIONS

As the night wore on, the red mare went slower, and slower yet, in silence, and with difficulty, for the snow lay ever deeper on their way. *Page 24*

"Trolls!" the mare shouted. "Trolls! Would you like a ride on the red mare's back?" *Pages 28–29*

From her coat pocket the girl pulled out the only weapon she had—one of the long, strong, wooden knitting needles her father had made. *Page 32*

Some of the troll-children pressed closer to the girl, jeering at her. One of them pulled her hair. Another one, squatting on the floor, tried to hold her by the ankle. *Page 35*

All the trolls pushed into a circle around the red mare, not standing close, for her hooves flashed and her teeth snapped. *Pages 38–39*

Sister and brother walked on and walked on, and as the sunlight died away and the air turned cold and blue, they came to the wooden bridge across the river. *Page 43*

"This is for you," the girl's father said. "I couldn't sleep, night or day, so I whittled, and this is what I made." *Page 47*

A RIDE ON THE RED MARE'S BACK

1

A long time ago, when the world was wild, a family lived in the forests of the North, far from any other house.

The father was going hunting, and he said, "I'll take the boy with me."

"The dark winter's coming," the mother said. "Listen to the wind!"

"Wrap him up warm," said the father.

"He's very young to hunt," she said.

"Old enough to learn," said the father, and he took down the little boy's warm coat and put it on him. "So," he said, "in a day or two we'll be back with meat!" He went out of the house, the little boy running ahead of him.

That night the dark winter came. The wind blew colder and colder, and snow whirled in the darkness.

When the baby was asleep, the mother sat down by the fire to sew. The eldest child, a girl, sat near her. She had just learned how to knit, and she was making a warm scarf for her little brother. She finished it that evening, and knotted the fringes, and held it up. "I wish he had it now!" she said.

"They'll be all right," the mother said. But they heard the cold wind blowing, and the snow beat against the walls all night.

When the sun rose, the air was still at last, and the fields were white, and the forest was black. Out of the forest came the father, walking slowly, alone. They ran to meet him.

"Where is our son?" the mother cried.

And the father answered, "Trolls took him."

He would say no more than that. He went into the house and sat by the fire, shivering. He would not speak. Only when the mother cried, "But where did you leave him?" he said again, "Trolls took him," and nothing more.

But there was a great bruise on his forehead, as if he had been struck down.

The daughter watched and listened. That night, sitting by the fire, she cried for her little brother, but she cried silently, because her father and mother were silent.

Her mother spoke once in a low voice: "Could you not follow him?" And the father, sitting by the fire, shook his head.

Next day while the girl worked, she watched and listened, but her mother and father said no word to each other at all.

She did her work in the house and in the barn, and when the cows were fed and the baby was asleep, she went to the bedroom in the loft, where they all slept. On the shelf by her bed was the only toy she had, a wooden horse that her father had carved and painted for her. It was a proud and stiff horse, standing on its four straight legs, painted bright shiny red. For bridle and saddle there were flowers painted on it.

In one coat pocket she put the scarf she had made for her brother, and the wooden knitting needles that her father had also made for her, and the rest of the ball of yarn. In the other coat pocket she put the end of a loaf of bread that her mother had baked that morning. She took the toy horse in her hand, and she said, "I'm going outside."

Her father stared into the fire and said nothing. Her mother said quietly, "Don't go too far."

Her mother's voice was like a fine, thin thread of silk or silver that lay behind her as she walked across the snowy fields and into the forest, looking for her brother who had been taken by the trolls.

2

Under the trees of the forest it was dark, but the air was clear, and the girl walked bravely along. She did not know much about trolls, only that they were dangerous and sometimes lived under bridges. She did not know which way through the forest her father had taken with the boy. She walked ahead on the path, and when the path branched, she said to the toy horse she carried, "Which way?"

The horse was in her left hand, so its head pointed left, and she went that way.

She walked on and walked on. She saw nothing but the tall dark trees, and a few birds flitting silently, and here and there in the thin snow the tracks of mice and rabbits, foxes and deer.

Days are short in the dark winter of the North. The yellow sunlight slanted through the trees and then was gone. The light was cold and blue.

"Oh, horse," said the girl, "should we go back home?"

The wooden horse kept looking straight ahead.

The girl walked on. She felt lonely, so she talked to the wooden horse. "Mother can't look for my brother," she said. "The baby is delicate, and she has to stay with it. So we should find the trolls and bring my brother home. But where shall we spend the night?"

The wooden horse kept looking at the path ahead of them, so she went on. The air grew lighter as the path led out of the forest to the bank of a river. The open sky above the water was still bright with evening. But the river ran swift and dark, and across it was a narrow wooden bridge.

The girl was afraid. She took a step forward and then stood still. She took one more step, and one more, and now she stood on the bridge. And over the side of the bridge, from underneath it, a great, long arm came reaching, and a great, wide hand groped toward her.

She held the toy horse tight in her hand and held still, whispering, "Oh, horse! Help me!"

She felt the wooden toy move in her hand. It quivered, and trembled, and then it leapt from her hand. As its wooden feet

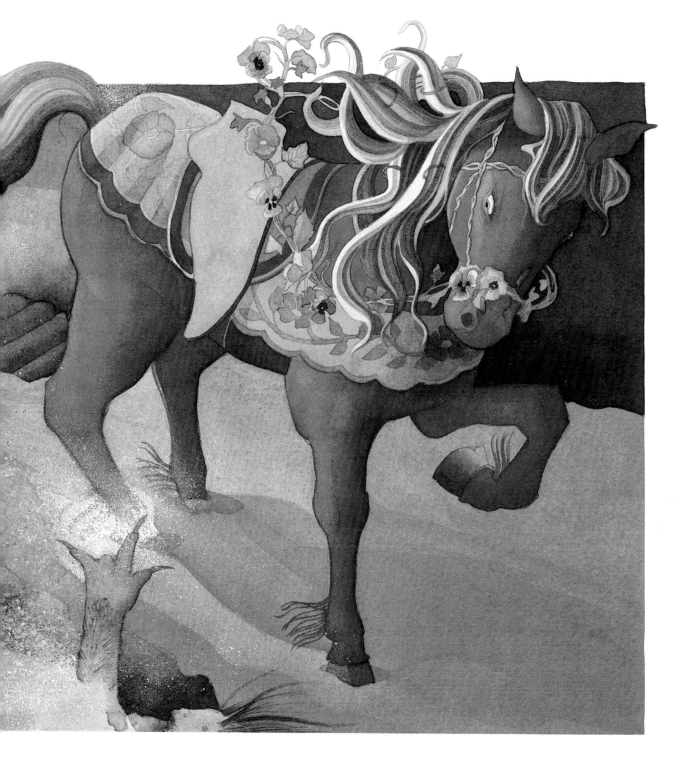

struck the bridge, they turned to hooves, and it stood upon them, a real horse, full size, bright red, with a bridle and saddle of flowers, and bright, fiery eyes!

The horse stamped on the planks. The huge arm drew back, and a voice shouted from underneath the bridge, "Who's that stamping on my bridge?"

"Me! The red mare!"

Then the girl and the red mare listened, and they heard the troll under the bridge bumping and banging about and swearing and having a tantrum.

"It's afraid of me," the red mare said to the girl with a snort, and she stamped on the planks again.

"Stop that!" the troll yelled. "Go on! Go across! Go away!"

"Mount on my back," said the red mare to the girl, and quickly she mounted onto the flower saddle and took up the reins that were a leafy vine.

There on the red mare's back she had no fear. She cried out, "Troll! Where did your brothers take my brother?"

The troll poked up his head from underneath the bridge, and, oh, he was an ugly troll, with eyes like snail's tracks.

"What'll you pay me if I tell you?" he growled.

"I'll give you my mother's bread," said the girl.

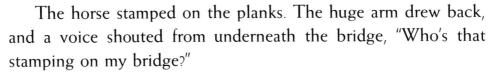

The troll reached up his horny, wide, hard hand again, and she put the bread in it.

"The boy's in the High House," growled the troll.

And as the red mare trotted on across the bridge, they could hear him underneath, biting and chewing the bread as if he had been starved for years.

3

"I know the way to the High House," the red mare said. "But it's a long way. We must come there tonight and bring your brother away before the dawn, for I have only this one night with you."

"My beautiful red mare," said the girl, "I should have saved the bread for you."

"That's not what I live on," said the mare. "Now, hold on, my girl!"

The red mare broke into a gallop, and as the night grew deeper she ran through the darkness like a flying spark. The girl clung to her, and though the wind was bitter cold and snow blew hard and blinding, yet she smelled the sweetness of flowers as they galloped on.

Sometimes stones clattered under the red mare's hooves, and sometimes the ice of a frozen lake rang like iron bells.

As the night wore on, the red mare went slower, and slower yet, in silence, and with difficulty, for the snow lay ever deeper on their way. At last she was pushing forward one step at a time, and the snow was up to her knees.

"Let me dismount," the girl said, but the red mare shook her head, saying, "The snow's too deep for you. Ride, and look ahead for the High House!"

So the girl gazed ahead into the darkness. And after a long or a short time she saw that the whirling snow glimmered in a dim light that shone far ahead and above them.

"There's a light," she whispered. The red mare bowed her neck and pushed on, climbing, one step at a time, though the snow was almost to her shoulders now.

She took one more step, and the snow was gone. She stood in a circle of light on a bare pavement before a stone door that stood open in the high side of a mountain. The snowy plain was behind them, and rocks and snow and cliffs in front of them, and the dark sky overhead.

"This is the High House," the red mare said, "where the trolls live."

The girl slipped from her back and stood beside her.

"Is my brother inside the mountain?" she asked.

The red mare nodded.

"Are there many trolls there?" she asked.

The red mare nodded.

"Are they afraid of you?" she asked.

The red mare shook her head. "But I'm not afraid of them!" she said, stamping her hoof and shaking her leafy bridle. "So this is what we'll do, my girl. I'll call out the trolls, and tease them, and make them angry. They'll try to catch me. And while they're chasing me, you'll slip inside the mountain and find your brother and bring him out. But you must bring him out before the sun rises, for the trolls will all go back underground at the first light of dawn, lest they be caught in the sunlight and turned to stone. And I have only this one night with you."

"But if they catch you—" cried the girl.

"They'll be sorry," said the red mare. "Now, when they come out, take your chance and slip in like a mouse."

Then the mare reared up on her hind legs and let out a great ringing neigh and came down stamping on her forehooves. "Trolls!" she shouted. "Trolls! Would you like a ride on the red mare's back?"

There was a sound of roaring and yelling inside the mountain. Trolls came pouring out of the door, dozens and scores of them, hairy and scaly and scowling, and, oh, they were ugly trolls. Their arms were long and their hands wide; their skins were white and

their eyes small. They came running out so fast, reaching for the red mare's reins, that she barely leapt away in time. She galloped up into the rocks and snow and darkness of the mountainside. Some of the trolls carried flaring torches, and all of them went running after her, shouting, "Catch her! Head her off! Catch her reins! Drive her to the cliff's edge!"

Then the girl crept like a mouse's shadow through that high door into the mountain.

4

Behind her she heard the shouting of the trolls. That noise died away. She stood in a silent stone corridor that led a long way into the mountain. At the far end of it shone a light.

She walked forward. The walls were rough and the roof was low and damp. Underfoot lay waste and rubbish. The air smelled foul. In a room that opened off the corridor, she saw a great heap of rotting food. In another room a broken chair leaned against a broken table. Rats scurried from her steps.

As she came nearer to the light at the end of the corridor, she saw that it came from a room where torches were set burning

about the walls. Voices shouted, shrill and harsh. She walked carefully, keeping in the shadows at the side of the corridor. She came to the doorway and peered in.

The room was huge, like a cave, and full of smoke from the torches. Around and across it children raced—troll-children, little ones and bigger ones, screaming and yelling, chasing and hitting, tripping and grabbing, throwing things, yanking things, breaking things. Under a sputtering torch, several large troll-children were twisting the arms of a smaller one to make it scream. On a pile of smashed toys and furniture one troll-child stood, bellowing, "I won! I'm king! I won!" Near the doorway two troll-babies, filthy dirty, sat shivering in a heap of wet rags, weeping in high voices. In the middle of the room a thin troll-child had made a fire of trash and was cooking something over it on a stick. And far across the room four or five troll-children were fighting over a toy of some kind, or perhaps something to eat. They were screaming and struggling and hitting one another. She looked at them and saw that one of them was not a troll-child, but her brother.

She forgot caution and started to go to him.

Just beside her, a deep, rough voice spoke: "Who goes there?"

The girl stopped in terror. A broad, tall, old, white troll squatted like a huge toad beside the doorway. It peered at her with its dim snail-track eyes, reaching out its hand to stop her.

From her coat pocket she pulled out the only weapon she had—one of the long, strong, wooden knitting needles her father had made. She held it ready to stab the troll's hand. But the troll did not try to seize her. It peered at her stupidly, and waited.

"I'm one of the children," she said.

"Oh," said the old troll. It stared at the knitting needle. "What's that?" it said.

"A knitting needle."

"What's that?"

"To knit with."

"What's that?"

"Don't you know? Like this." The girl pulled out the other needle and the ball of yarn and showed them to the old troll. It peered at them.

"Do it," it said.

"Well, you cast on, like this. And then you knit, like this. You see?"

"Yes, yes," the old troll said. "I can do that. I have to sit here and keep the children from running away. I hate sitting here. I hate children. Give me that!"

The girl put the needles and yarn into the creature's wide, hard hand. It waved the needles around and tried to make a stitch.

"If you did it this way—" said the girl, but the old troll was too stupid and impatient to listen to her. "I know how!" it growled, and it went on winding the yarn around the needles and making knots and tangles. It was quite busy, so she ran across the cave room straight to her little brother and caught him by the hand. "Come on, come quick!" she said.

But he stared at her and pulled his hand away. He stuck out his tongue. "What are *you* here for?" he shouted.

Several troll-children gathered around, showing the teeth in their wide mouths. They imitated him, shouting, "What are *you* here for?"

"Brother, come with me," she said.

"Why should I? I like it here!"

"Mother and Father are grieving for you."

"I don't care. I like it here. I can do anything I like here. I don't ever go to bed. I can eat rats! I can kick people! I'm going to be a troll when I grow up, and be stronger than anybody, and kill things!"

Some of the troll-children pressed closer to her, jeering at her. One of them pulled her hair. Another one, squatting on the floor, tried to hold her by the ankle. She looked at her little brother, and, oh, he was as ugly as a troll, showing his teeth at her.

"Come with me," she said, but he shouted, "No!"

She turned and went back across the room toward the doorway. There the old troll squatted, making a mighty tangle with the yarn. It had noticed nothing. It scratched its head with a knitting needle and made another knot. The girl put her hand in her pocket and felt the scarf she had knitted for her brother. She turned and walked back through the yelling, running, fighting troll-children to her brother. He stood quite alone, looking small.

"I made this for you," she said, and held out the scarf.

"It's cold here," he said. He took the scarf and wrapped it around his neck, hunching his shoulders. "I'm cold," he said. "I want to go home."

"Come on," she said, but he stood there with his shoulders hunched and did not move. She picked him up, and he put his arms around her neck. She carried him across the cave room, right past the old troll, who had now made all the yarn into one huge knot and was jabbing at it with the needles.

She carried her brother down the long corridor, hurrying, for she could see that outside the door of the mountain it was no longer night. Dawn was coming, and the air was pale. She carried

her brother through the door and into the open air, and there she set him down. He stood beside her, holding her hand.

5

The girl turned and looked up the mountainside. Plunging down the steep slopes came the red mare. Ropes dangled from her neck, ropes flew from her legs, and a horde of trolls ran and leapt and hopped alongside her, snatching at the ropes. "We've got her!" they shouted. "Now! Catch her! She's caught!"

A huge troll caught the end of the rope around the red mare's neck and pulled her aside. Another grabbed her reins and stopped her, though she kicked and plunged and nearly broke free.

All the trolls pushed into a circle around her, not standing close, for her hooves flashed and her teeth snapped. But the biggest troll came closer to her from behind, holding a long stone knife.

"Look out!" the girl cried, and the red mare whirled and reared up—and at that instant the sun's first ray shone bright across the snowy land, striking full on the red mare and the circle of trolls.

Dazzled, the girl rubbed her eyes. When she looked again, she saw on the mountainside a circle of great standing stones.

In the midst of the stones a little red thing lay on the snow.

Holding her brother's hand tight, she ran in among the stones and picked up her toy horse. Its paint was chipped and one shoulder was battered, but it was not broken.

"Oh, my beautiful red mare," the girl whispered, and she kissed

it. Then, holding it in her left hand and her brother's hand in her right, she turned and said, "Now we must go home."

"Where is home?" asked the little boy.

They stood on the side of the mountain in the sunrise. Before them all was wilderness: white snow, grey rock, black forest.

But down the slopes of the mountain, across the snowy plain, reaching into the forest, lay a thin, fine, silvery thread, delicate as spiderweb.

"This way," the girl said.

And they set off, following the silvery thread.

A long way they had to go. They saw only a few birds flitting in the forest trees, and the tracks of mice and rabbits, foxes and deer, in the snow. But the sun shone, and the wind was mild. They found a nut tree that still bore good nuts, and drank from a spring among icy ferns. They walked on and walked on, and as the sunlight died away and the air turned cold and blue, they came to the wooden bridge across the river.

"Oh," cried the little boy, "this is where the trolls came and took me from my father!"

He did not want to set foot on the planks of the bridge, but his sister held his hand and said, "Come on. Don't be afraid. This troll is our friend now."

They walked across the bridge, their feet going *trip! trap!* on the planks. But all the troll underneath the bridge said was, "Good bread!"

"You're welcome," said the girl, and she and her brother went on.

Though it was dark in the forest now, the silvery thread glimmered before them, showing the way. And after a long time or a short time, they saw the firelight in the windows of their house, shining across the snow.

When they came into the house, the baby was sleeping in the mother's lap. Both the parents sat awake by the fire, late as it was, deep in the night. The father stared at them as if he thought he was dreaming. The mother took them in her arms and held them close. She kissed them, and heated milk for them, and made them sit close to the fire. The father and mother listened to them tell where they had been and what they had done. Then the mother tucked the little boy into his bed, for he was half-asleep already. She held the girl to her once again, whispering, "My brave daughter!"

Her father, sitting by the fire, held something out to her.

"This is for you," he said. "I couldn't sleep, night or day, so I whittled, and this is what I made."

It was a tiny wooden horse, not half as big as the red mare. It was not painted, but it stood proud and stiff on its four straight legs.

"It is the red mare's colt," the girl said.

"I'll paint it tomorrow," said her father.

She kissed her father and her mother good-night. She took the colt and set it by the red mare on the shelf above the bed, so they stood side by side.

When she slept that night, she dreamed how the red mare
would run with her colt through grass and flowers in the sunlight
in the spring, their hooves striking
sparks from stones, and the
wild wind blowing.